WITHDRAWN

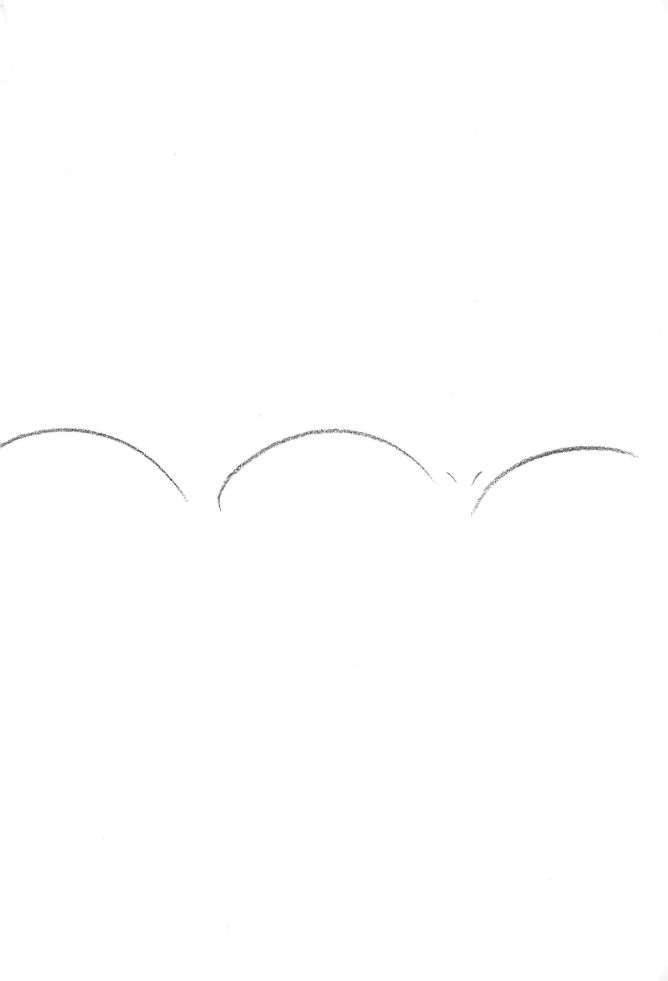

In memory of Palpary (the real heroine of the book), and Yeppi (her daughter) and to Damy and Hwajung.

First American Edition 2003 by Kane/Miller Book Publishers
La Jolla, California

Originally published under the title "What on Earth Happened During that Time?"
by Jaimimage Publishing Co., Ltd., Seoul, Korea

Text and Illustrations Copyright © by Ho Baek Lee

Library of Congress Control Number: 2002112325

Printed and bound in Hong Kong by Phoenix Asia

2 3 4 5 6 7 8 9 10

ISBN 1-929132-44-1

While We Were Out

By Ho Baek Lee

Kane/Miller
BOOK PUBLISHERS

The apartment is quiet. They've all gone to Grandma's house.
There is somebody on the balcony though.

Who forgot to lock the door? A little push, and...

...the rabbit is inside.

She's hungry. What looks good?

She sits at the table to eat, just as the family does.

They won't be back until morning.
Now is her chance to watch a movie.

Then it's time to explore.
She hops onto the dressing table, picks up this, smells that,
a touch of lipstick … "beautiful," she thinks.

She finds a colorful costume.
The youngest in the family wore it to her first birthday party.
It fits perfectly.

The next room is full of books.
The rabbit opens one, but she doesn't understand it.

She goes to another room instead.
There are lots of toys. She builds a robot with blocks…

. . .and fishes with magnets.

There are interesting things in the closet, too. Even skates!
The rabbit has wanted to try them for a long time.

They're much too big though.

She hops to the kitchen…

…and finds just what she is looking for.

(What will she do with those chopsticks?)

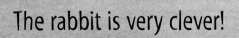

The rabbit is very clever!

She's getting tired. She's had a busy day.

It's early morning when the sun wakes her.
The family will be home soon.

The rabbit hops back to her balcony,

closes the door,

and lies down as if nothing unusual has happened.

She's had a wonderful adventure, and the family will never know.

Or will they?